TALE OF THE
RIBLE TEETH

First published in Great Britain 1996 by Heinemann Young Books
an imprint of Reed International Books Limited.
Michelin House, 81 Fulham Rd, London SW3 6RB
Mammoth paperback edition first published 1998
Published in hardback by Heinemann Educational Publishers,
a division of Reed Educational and Professional Publishing Limited
by arrangement with Reed International Books Limited.
Text copyright © Hazel Townson 1996
Illustrations copyright © Russell Ayto 1996
The Author and Illustrator have asserted their moral rights
Paperback ISBN 0 7497 3509 0
Hardback ISBN 0 434 80368 5
10 9 8 7 6 5 4
A CIP catalogue record for this title is available from the British Library
Printed at Oriental Press Limited, Dubai

HAZEL TOWNSON

THE TALE OF THE TERRIBLE TEETH

ILLUSTRATED BY RUSSELL AYTO

 YELLOW BANANAS

For my new granddaughter Clea,
born in Paris, November 16th 1995.

Chapter One
DISASTER IN THE SAND

THIS IS GARY and his mum and dad and grandpa.

They went to Egypt for their holidays.

Grandpa opened his mouth to gape at the
pyramids . . .

and dropped his false teeth in the sand.

Those teeth instantly sank out of sight and were never seen again.

So Grandpa bought some more teeth in the
Bizarre Bazaar that sold everything from
wooden legs to cotton cosies for camels'
humps.

Were those new teeth any good? Well, they could bite all right. They could even chew through glue without getting stuck up. But the trouble was they chattered.

'So what?' you might say. 'Teeth *do* chatter if you're cold or scared.' But you don't get cold in hot and steamy Egypt. And Gary's grandpa was a retired all-in wrestler who had never been scared in his life.

Gary and Grandpa shared a bedroom at the Fuzzy Fez Hotel and it was there, in the middle of the night, that the teeth first started chattering. Grandpa had put them in a glass of vile Nile water on his bedside table before he went to sleep. But just after midnight Gary was woken by a funny glugging sound coming from the glass.

Grandpa's teeth seemed to be blowing bubbles!

They were making such a noise that Gary took them out of the glass and set them down on a nice, clean hanky. Whereupon the teeth said:

Thanks very much. You have no idea how difficult it is to chatter under water, especially through all that pollution.

Gary was more shaken than a spring-cleaner's duster. He stuck his horrified head underneath the sheet . . .

But that didn't save him from the terrors of Chapter Two.

Chapter Two
THE CHATTY CHOPPERS

'YOU'LL HAVE HEARD of Cheops,' the teeth
continued chattily. 'He was the Pharaoh who
built The Great Pyramid. Everybody's heard of

him. Well we're Cheops'. choppers, and we've spent so long in that scruffy old sarcophagus that we thought it was time we came out for a bite to eat.'

What sort of bite? wondered Gary in horror. He tried stuffing the sheet into his ears to drown out the chattering, but it made no difference.

'So bring out the refreshments!' Cheops' choppers went on. 'We've been starving for centuries and we need to sink ourselves into something tasty.'

Right *now!*

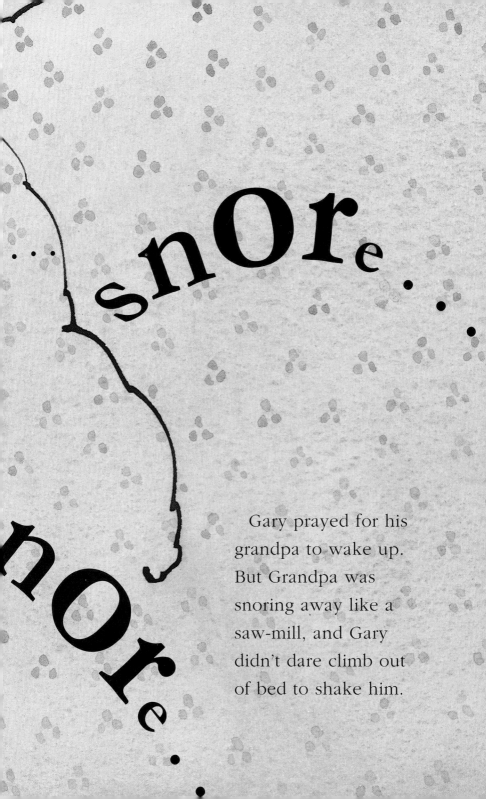

snore...

snore...

Gary prayed for his grandpa to wake up. But Grandpa was snoring away like a saw-mill, and Gary didn't dare climb out of bed to shake him.

'You must understand,' chattered the teeth, 'that being part of a Pharaoh, we are used to being waited on hand and foot, so you'd better hurry up and fetch us a nice, filling feast or face the consequences.'

That did it! Gary reached out of bed,
grabbed the telephone, dialled Room Service
and asked for a five-course meal for two.

'Sorry, sir!' said a
snooty voice, 'but the
kitchen staff are
refusing to serve
dinner after midnight.
In fact they have just
walked out on
strike.'

Which left Gary in real trouble in Chapter Three.

Chapter Three
TAKE-AWAY TROUBLE

WHEN GARY EXPLAINED about the strike, the teeth went snapping mad.

They clacked like castanets across Gary's bed,
making straight for his meaty cheeks.

'Stop! Wait!' yelled Gary, leaping out of bed
at last. 'Just give me five minutes and I'll run
round to the Tutankhamun Take-away. They'll
serve you a super supper.'

He grabbed
Grandpa's
wallet and fled
still wearing
his stripy
pyjamas
which,
however, blended well with the local street gear.

But alas! The police had just been to take away the Take-away because the Shish-Kebab queue had been causing a frisky babble, which had turned into a riotous rabble and blocked all the traffic.

First no Room Service, and now no Take-away! Things were looking desperate.

Gary ran on in panic. He must find some food for Cheops' choppers.

Then suddenly, as he by-passed a passer-by, he noticed she was carrying a basket of dates on her head. Gary thought that was clever.

He couldn't even carry dates *in* his head, never mind out on top.

But at least he was clever enough to see the answer to his problem.

Bargaining with a bunch of Grandpa's fivers, Gary bought the dates, basket and all. But he got more than he'd bargained for. That heavy basket had more dates in it than a ten-year diary. It took all Gary's strength to stagger back to the Fuzzy Fez Hotel with the load. Still, it was worth all the trouble. Just wait until the ravenous teeth got stuck into that lot!

Yet, when Gary reached his room, he had a dreadful shock. The terrible teeth were gone . . . and so was Grandpa! There were just a few strange-looking crumbs on the floor.

Were those crumbs a gruesome clue to the contents of Chapter Four?

Chapter Four
A RUDE AWAKENING

GARY DUMPED THE dates and ran to his parents' room.

'Mum! Dad!' he yelled. 'Wake up! Cheops'
choppers have eaten Grandpa!'

'Eh? What?' yawned Gary's dad.

'You've been dreaming!' grumbled Gary's
mum. 'I told you not to eat that great big
chocolate Sphinx on top of your supper.'

'Honest, Mum, I'm telling the truth! Those teeth were starving hungry. They were going to eat me if I hadn't run off to get them some proper food, but when I got back I found Grandpa had vanished. If you don't believe me, come and look.'

Gary's mum peered at Gary. He certainly looked panic-stricken but he also looked wide awake. Maybe the boy was not dreaming after all.

'Come on, then!' Mum cried, shaking Gary's dad awake and grabbing her dressing-gown. 'Best take a look!'

Well, as soon as Gary's parents saw that Grandpa really had vanished,

they fetched the Hotel Manager.

He then fetched the police.

The police wasted no time. A full-scale search of the premises began. Guests were rudely woken up, wardrobe doors were flung open,

balconies were searched. Curtains were pulled apart and the contents of large suitcases were tipped onto the floor.

It was chaos! And it might have got even worse if a cross-looking Grandpa hadn't suddenly marched in from the street!

So where will those teeth turn up in Chapter Five?

Chapter Five

THE LAST LONG DROP

'WHERE HAVE YOU *been*?' cried Gary's mum.
'We've turned this place upside-down
searching for you.'

'You're supposed to be fast asleep in bed,' grumbled Grandpa. 'Anyway, I should hope I'm entitled to go looking for my wallet. I woke up and found it had gone. That's enough to get anybody out of bed. Either I had lost it outside or somebody had pinched it.'

'Grandpa - y-you've got your t-teeth in!' stammered Gary, aghast.

'Course I have!' said Grandpa. 'You don't think I'd go out in the street without 'em, do you? I have my pride, even in the middle of the night.'

'Well, go back to bed
for goodness' sake,'
nagged Gary's mum.
'You've nearly started a
riot in this hotel. We'll look
for your wallet in the
morning.'

As they all climbed into the rickety lift to go back to their rooms, Gary thought with relief:

At least Grandpa's all in one piece. Perhaps it was a nightmare after all. Anyway, we'll soon find out when he takes his teeth out again.

Gary felt as if the whole weight of the pyramids might just be about to shift off his shoulders.

But then, as the ill-fitting lift gates jerked open and Gary stepped out in front of Grandpa, the old man shouted: 'Here! What's that sticking out of your pyjama pocket, young Gary?'

Grandpa opened his mouth so wide in angry surprise that his teeth fell down the lift-shaft and were never seen again.

Now nobody will ever know the truth about those terrible teeth . . .

unless somebody writes Chapter Six.